STEM IN THE SUMMER OLYMPICS
THE SCIENCE BEHIND WATER SPORTS

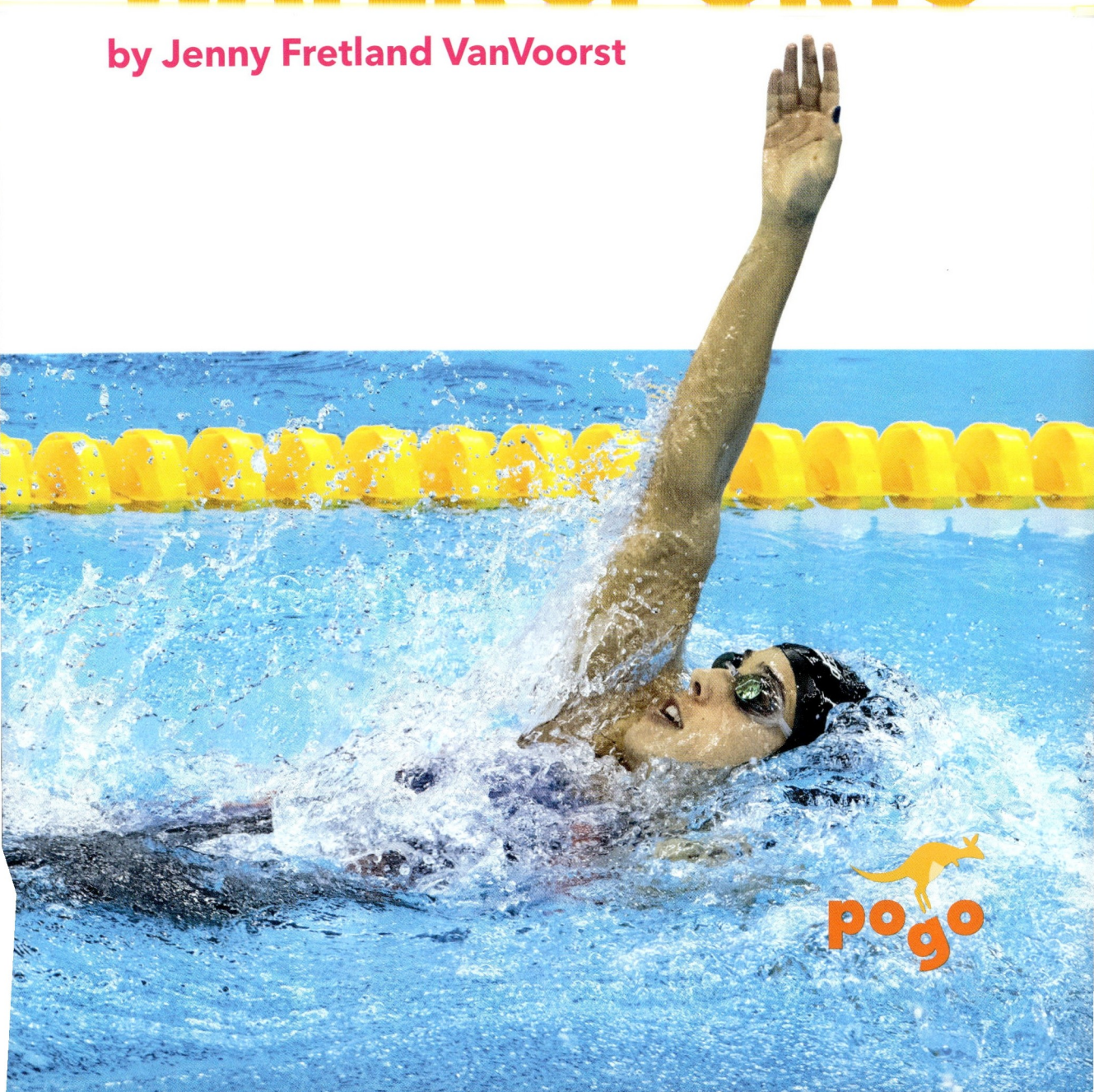

by Jenny Fretland VanVoorst

Ideas for Parents and Teachers

Pogo Books let children practice reading informational text while introducing them to nonfiction features such as headings, labels, sidebars, maps, and diagrams, as well as a table of contents, glossary, and index.

Carefully leveled text with a strong photo match offers early fluent readers the support they need to succeed.

Before Reading

- "Walk" through the book and point out the various nonfiction features. Ask the student what purpose each feature serves.
- Look at the glossary together. Read and discuss the words.

Read the Book

- Have the child read the book independently.
- Invite him or her to list questions that arise from reading.

After Reading

- Discuss the child's questions. Talk about how he or she might find answers to those questions.
- Prompt the child to think more. Ask: Swimmers wear tight swimsuits to reduce drag. Can you think of another sport in which athletes want to reduce drag?

Pogo Books are published by Jump!
5357 Penn Avenue South
Minneapolis, MN 55419
www.jumplibrary.com

Copyright © 2020 Jump!
International copyright reserved in all countries. No part of this book may be reproduced in any form without written permission from the publisher.

Library of Congress Cataloging-in-Publication Data

Names: Fretland VanVoorst, Jenny, 1972- author.
Title: The science behind water sports / by Jenny Fretland VanVoorst.
Description: Pogo Books Edition.
Minneapolis, Minnesota: Pogo Books are published by Jump!, [2020] | Series: STEM in the Summer Olympics
Includes index.
Identifiers: LCCN 2019009427 (print)
LCCN 2019010966 (ebook)
ISBN 9781641289191 (ebook)
ISBN 9781641289177 (hardcover: alk. paper)
Subjects: LCSH: Aquatic sports—Juvenile literature.
Sports sciences—Juvenile literature.
Olympics—Juvenile literature.
Classification: LCC GV770.5 (ebook)
LCC GV770.5 .F74 2020 (print) | DDC 797—dc23
LC record available at https://lccn.loc.gov/2019009427

Editor: Susanne Bushman
Designer: Michelle Sonnek

Photo Credits: Tatiana Popova/Shutterstock, cover (clipboard); Anton Starikov/Shutterstock, cover (cap); homi/Shutterstock, cover (goggles); PCN Photography/Alamy, 1, 10-11; CTK/Alamy, 3; Leonard Zhukovsky/Shutterstock, 4, 17; The Asahi Shimbun/Getty, 5; Johannes Eisele/Getty, 6-7; PA Images/Alamy, 8-9; Brazil Photo Press/Getty, 12; Carl de Souza/Getty, 13; Xinhua/Alamy, 14-15; dpa picture alliance/Alamy, 16; Aflo Co. Ltd./Alamy, 18-19; ITAR-TASS News Agency/Alamy, 20-21; CP DC Press/Shutterstock, 23.

Printed in the United States of America at Corporate Graphics in North Mankato, Minnesota.

TABLE OF CONTENTS

CHAPTER 1
Thrust and Speed 4

CHAPTER 2
Gravity and Buoyancy 12

CHAPTER 3
In Motion 16

ACTIVITIES & TOOLS
Try This! 22
Glossary 23
Index 24
To Learn More 24

CHAPTER 1

THRUST AND SPEED

Dive in! There are many ways to enjoy the water. Just look at the Olympics. It has many water events. Like what? Swimming. Diving.

synchronized swimming

Synchronized swimming. Boat racing. Water polo, too!

CHAPTER 1 5

Water makes sports fun. It can make them harder, too. Water is about 800 times **denser** than air. It takes more **energy** to move through it. Olympic athletes must overcome this. They think about **forces** to win big!

CHAPTER 1

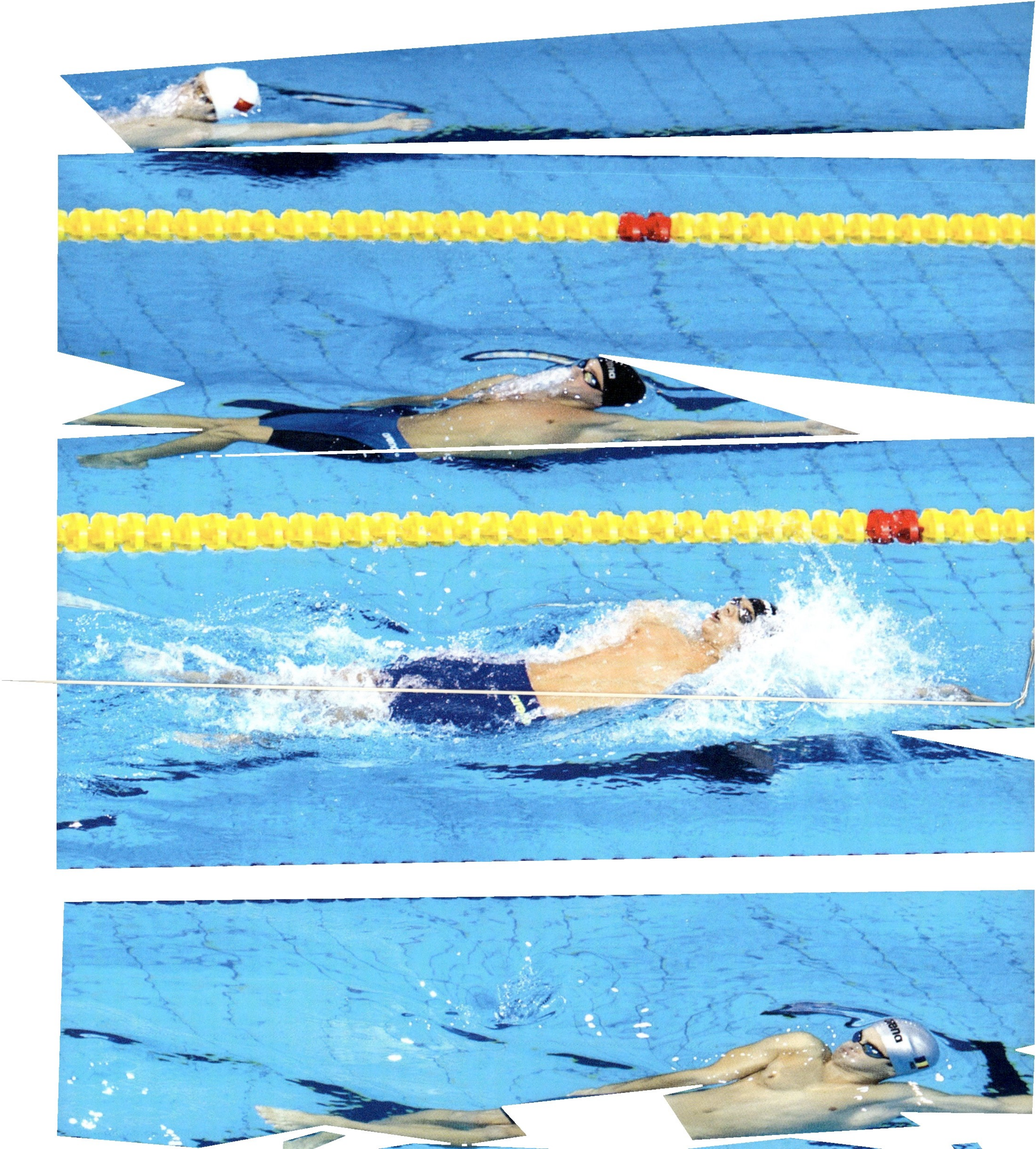

oar

CHAPTER 1

Row! This athlete races through the water. **Thrust** pushes him forward in the water with each row. More thrust means more speed. Canoers, kayakers, and rowers apply this to their paddles and oars. For sailors, this force comes from the wind. Swimmers create this with their strokes.

DID YOU KNOW?

There are four different Olympic swimming strokes. What are they? Freestyle. Backstroke. Breaststroke. And butterfly.

CHAPTER 1 | 9

CHAPTER 1

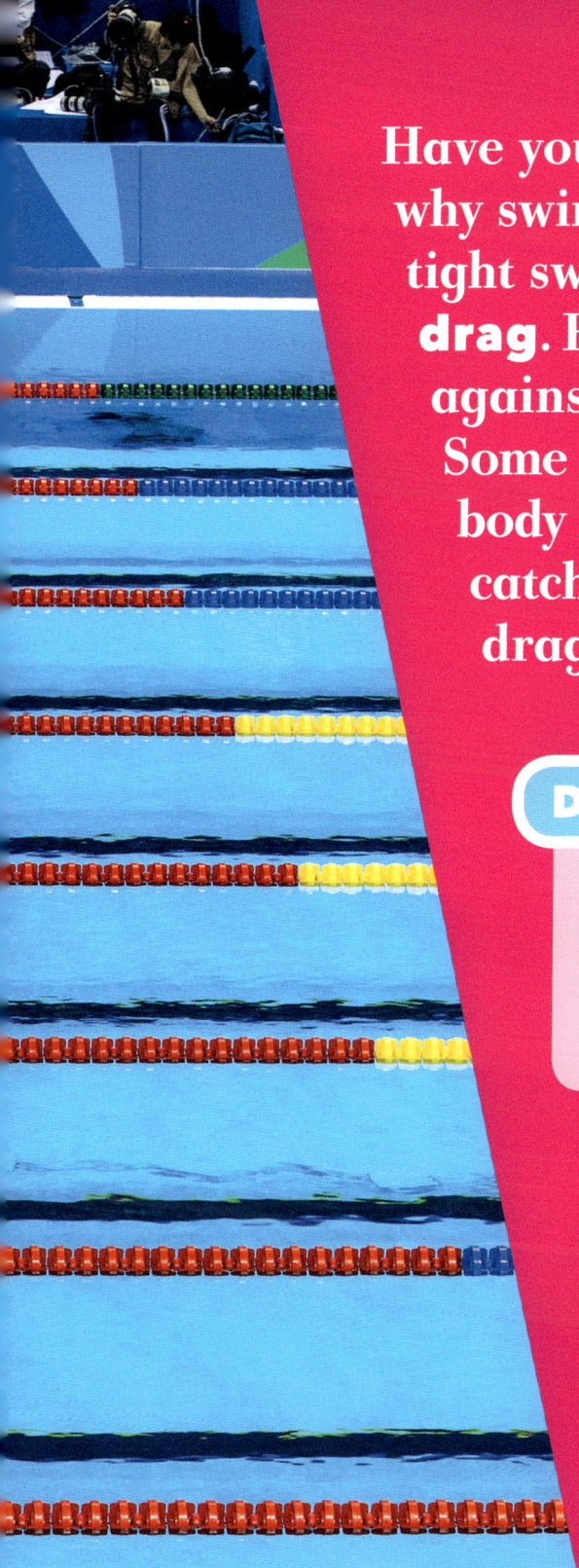

Have you ever wondered why swimmers wear caps and tight swimsuits? These prevent **drag**. How? Water does not drag against hair or loose material. Some swimmers also shave their body hair. Why? So water cannot catch against it. This reduces drag even more.

DID YOU KNOW?

Swimming was part of the first modern Olympics in 1896. It has been part of every summer games since. There are more than 30 different swimming events!

CHAPTER 1

CHAPTER 2
GRAVITY AND BUOYANCY

Gravity pulls swimmers toward the bottom of a body of water. It pulls divers down from the diving board.

Buoyancy works against gravity. Objects float in water. But only when their buoyancy is greater than the gravity that pulls on them.

CHAPTER 2　13

Olympians balance buoyancy and gravity. At the same time, they increase thrust and reduce drag. What is the result? Increased speed! This is how Olympians win gold!

CHAPTER 2

TAKE A LOOK!

Many forces affect swimmers. See how they work together!

gravity

thrust

drag

buoyancy

CHAPTER 2 15

CHAPTER 3
IN MOTION

Zoom! Watch the canoer race by. How does he create thrust? He moves his paddle in the opposite direction he wants to go. Swimmers do the same with their arms. Why?

It is a **law of motion**. Every action creates an equal and opposite reaction. Pulling the water back pushes a body forward.

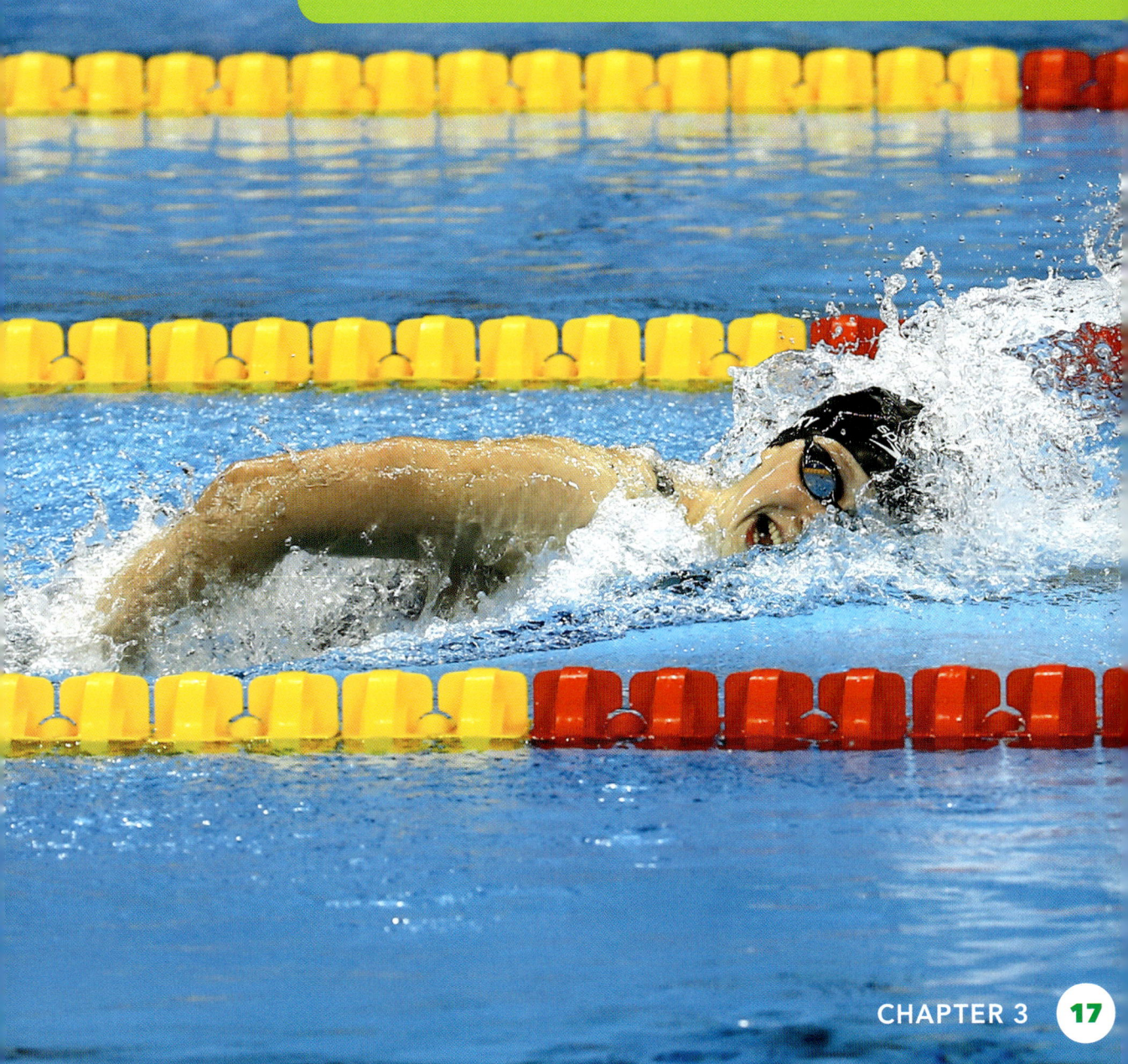

CHAPTER 3

water polo

Some Olympians use **lift**. Lift works against gravity. Water polo players push water down. This lifts them up and out of the water. It sets them up for a throw. Lift helps synchronized swimmers, too.

DID YOU KNOW?

It is illegal to touch the bottom of the pool in some sports. Which ones? Synchronized swimming and water polo.

CHAPTER 3

Divers push off from a platform. Their feet **exert** a downward force. The force is returned upward. It sends the divers into the air! The harder they push off, the higher they fly. They have more time in the air to twist and spin.

Olympians are strong. They use **physics** to win medals. Can you use science during your next trip to the pool?

CHAPTER 3

ACTIVITIES & TOOLS

TRY THIS!

BUILD YOUR OWN BOAT

How do buoyancy and gravity interact? Try this activity to find out!

What You Need:
- a paper plate
- scissors
- tape
- a sink or tub filled with water
- a handful of pennies or other small coins

❶ Use your paper plate, scissors, and tape to create a small boat. Cover any holes with tape so water cannot get in.

❷ Float your boat in the water.

❸ Add one penny to the boat. Does the boat sink lower into the water?

❹ Continue adding pennies one by one. How many pennies can your boat hold before it starts to sink?

❺ Make a change to your boat, such as making it wider or deeper. Does this affect how many pennies your boat can hold?

❻ Continue making changes one by one. What is the most buoyant boat you can make?

GLOSSARY

buoyancy: The upward force of water that pushes on objects in the water.

denser: Thicker.

drag: The force that slows or blocks motion or advancement.

energy: The ability or strength to do things without getting tired.

exert: To use power to make something happen.

forces: Actions that produce, stop, or change the shape of movements or objects.

gravity: The force that pulls objects toward the center of Earth and keeps them from floating away.

law of motion: One of the three laws of physics that govern moving objects, such as every action has an equal and opposite reaction, that was discovered by Isaac Newton.

lift: The upward force that opposes the pull of gravity.

physics: The science that deals with matter, energy, and their interactions.

thrust: The force that drives a person or object forward.

INDEX

arms 16
boat racing 5
buoyancy 13, 14, 15
canoers 9, 16
divers 12, 20
diving 4
drag 11, 14, 15
energy 6
events 4, 11
forces 6, 9, 15, 20
gravity 12, 13, 14, 15, 19
kayakers 9
law of motion 17
lift 19
oars 9
paddles 9, 16
rowers 9
sailors 9
speed 9, 14
strokes 9
swimming 4, 9, 11, 15, 16
synchronized swimming 5, 19
thrust 9, 14, 15, 16
water polo 5, 19

TO LEARN MORE

Finding more information is as easy as 1, 2, 3.

1. Go to www.factsurfer.com
2. Enter "sciencebehindwatersports" into the search box.
3. Choose your book to see a list of websites.